趣味漫畫學英語

IDIOMS AND PHRASES
中英成語
有文化

Elaine Tin 著

crocodile tears

貓哭老鼠

新雅文化事業有限公司
www.sunya.com.hk

Contents 目錄

你想知道嗎？

Don't judge me by my cover!
請翻閱第 14-15 頁。

壞心腸的書

I cry crocodile tears when I eat my friend.
請翻閱第 24-25 頁。

吃同伴的鱷魚

Don't get cold feet when you come near me.
請翻閱第 26-27 頁。

攻擊小孩的怪獸

I'm looking for a needle in a haystack...
請翻閱第 12-13 頁。

找不到針的小孩

文化對照篇

由於中西文化各不相同，有些成語即使是表達相同的意思，中文和英文卻會採用不同的文字！

easy as pie 易如反掌

形容事情非常容易做到。

1. Swimming is **easy as pie**. You just need to practise more.
   游泳是一件很容易的事，你只需要多加練習。

2. We cleaned up the kitchen in an hour; it's **easy as pie**.
   我們只花了一小時就把廚房清潔好，真是易如反掌。

A: How did your maths exam go?

B: It was easy as pie. I got 100 marks.

A: Good for you!

多學一點

- 其他說法：easy as ABC / anything

- simple (adj.) 簡單的

- success (n.) 成功

- achieve (v.) 達到

rain cats
and dogs

傾盆大雨

形容雨下得又大又急。

1. It sometimes **rains cats and dogs** in summer.
   夏季時，偶爾會下起傾盆大雨。

2. It **rained cats and dogs** in the middle of the game.
   比賽期間下起傾盆大雨。

Ⓐ: Look! It's raining cats and dogs.

Ⓑ: Oh, too bad! We can't go out.

Ⓐ: No, we'd better stay home.

多學一點

- drizzle (v.) 下毛毛雨

- pour (v.) 傾瀉

- wet (adj.) 濕漉漉的

- drench (v.) 使（人）濕透

形容極受寵愛，受到珍視的人。

1. Chloe is **the apple of her grandpa's eye** – she is so adorable and sweet.
   可怡既可愛又親切，怪不得成了她爺爺的掌上明珠。

2. Mr. Wong has three kids, but his youngest daughter is **the apple of his eye**.
   黃先生有三個孩子，而他最喜愛的則是小女兒。

Ⓐ: Lucy is so helpful.

Ⓑ: Yes. She is so smart, too.

Ⓐ: I see why she is the apple of her class teacher's eye.

多學一點

- spoil (v.) 寵愛、溺愛

- cherish (v.) 鍾愛

- proud (adj.) 自豪的

* "gonna" 是 "going to" 的非正式說法。

英VS中

形容東西很難找到，或事情難以完成。

1. To find a key in this messy room is just like looking for a needle in a haystack.
   要在這雜亂的房間裏找鑰匙，簡直是大海撈針。

2. Stop searching for your necklace on the beach; you are just looking for a needle in a haystack.
   不要在沙灘裏找你的項鏈了，這根本是大海撈針。

妙語連場

A: What are you doing?

B: I am looking for a letter. I have no idea where I put it.

A: It's like looking for a needle in a haystack. Let me help you.

- search (v.) 搜尋

- locate (v.) 確認位置

- lose (v.) 丟失

13

judge a book by its cover

以貌取人

指根據外表判斷一個人好壞，就如同以封面來決定書好不好看。

1. That ragged man owns three houses in town. You should never **judge a book by its cover**.
   那衣衫襤褸的人在市內擁有三座房子，真是不能以貌取人。

2. The restaurant is nicely decorated, but the food is terrible. You can't **judge a book by its cover**!
   這間餐廳看上去很好，但食物卻很糟糕，真是「人不可貌相，海水不可斗量」！

妙語連場

A: He is our new team leader.

B: He looks clumsy. Look at his belly!

A: Don't judge a book by its cover. He was nominated for best player last year.

多學一點

- prejudge (v.) 未了解清楚便判斷

- outward (adj.) 外表的

形容機會極為難得，非常罕見。

1. **Once in a blue moon**, my little brother is reading a book quietly.
   小弟弟竟然靜靜地看書，真是千載難逢！

2. My uncle works overseas and he visits us **once in a blue moon**.
   叔叔在海外工作，很難得才探望我們一次。

妙語連場

A: I am overweight. I think I need to start exercising.

B: You need to do it regularly. It is useless if you exercise once in a blue moon.

A: You're right.

多學一點

- special (adj.) 特別的

- often (adv.) 經常

see the light 茅塞頓開

表示閉塞的思路清晰起來，忽然把問題想通了，明白過來。

1. After trying many times, Johnny finally **saw the light** about how to build this model.
經過多番嘗試，尊尼終於茅塞頓開，知道該如何砌這模型了。

2. **Seeing the light**, Dad finally found out how to fix the bicycle.
爸爸恍然大悟，終於想到如何維修這輛單車。

Ⓐ : Why do you look so annoyed?

Ⓑ : I can't solve this maths problem.

Ⓐ : Don't worry! You'll see the light soon.

多學一點

- problem (n.) 困難、難題

- suddenly (adv.) 突然

- realise (v.) 明白

19

time flies

光陰似箭

20

形容時間過得極快，就像
射出的箭快速飛過空中！

1. **Time flies** when I'm playing football with my friends.
   當我跟朋友一起踢足球，時間似箭一般溜走。

2. It's hard to believe we have been in this drama club for five years – **time flies**!
   想不到我們已待在這話劇學會五年，真是光陰似箭！

妙語連場

Ⓐ: Who's this little boy?

Ⓑ: This is my brother, Joe.

Ⓐ: Wow! He was still a baby when I saw him last time.

Ⓑ: Yea. Time flies.

多學一點

- pass (v.) 過去、流逝

- dawdle (v.) 拖延

- speedy (adj.) 迅速的

a drop in the bucket 九牛一毛

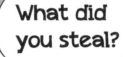

magic water

形容多數中極小的一部分，少得不值一提。

1. I have been doing my homework all day but it's just **a drop in the bucket**.

   我整天都在做功課，但完成了的就如九牛一毛。

2. The housework we do is **a drop in the bucket** compared to what Mom does.

   相比起媽媽，我們做的家務實在是九牛一毛。

A : Are you sure you want to donate all your savings to the charity?

B : Yes. That organisation helps many homeless people. What I give is just a drop in the bucket.

A : That's so kind of you.

多學一點

- lack (v.) 缺少

- insufficient (adj.) 不足夠的

23

crocodile tears 貓哭老鼠

形容人的憐憫只是裝出來，如同兇殘的鱷魚流下同情淚，不過是虛情假意。

1. Andy said he felt bad that we lost the game; he was just shedding **crocodile tears**.
   安迪說他替我們比賽落敗而難過，這根本就是貓哭老鼠。

2. She's pretending to feel bad. I don't believe her **crocodile tears**.
   她只是假裝難過，我不會相信她的眼淚，那只是貓哭老鼠而已。

A : I was punished by Miss Lee and she asked me to clean the classroom on my own.

B : Oh, poor you. I wish I could help you.

A : Ha ha! Stop crying crocodile tears.

多學一點

- hypocritical (adj.) 虛偽的

- sympathy (n.) 同情心

get cold feet 裹足不前

ROAR

My feet are wrapped... I can't move.

I got cold feet... I can't move, either.

HAHA!

英 vs 中

形容因害怕或有顧慮而停止不前，就像腳被纏住或麻痺了一樣，無法前進。

1. Danny **got cold feet** when his friends were diving into the water.
   丹尼的朋友都跳進水裏去了，他還裹足不前。

2. Jason's **getting cold feet** about joining the drama club – he is very shy.
   祖信對參加話劇學會一事猶豫不決，因為他實在太害羞了。

妙語連場

Ⓐ: I am so excited about our magic show tomorrow.

Ⓑ: But I've got cold feet; I am not quite ready for it.

Ⓐ: Don't worry. Let's practise once more.

多學一點

- nervous (adj.) 緊張的

- fearful (adj.) 恐懼的

- hesitate (v.) 猶疑

talk through one's hat　信口開河

形容不經思考，隨意亂說。

1. He keeps telling people that the president of the US is his good friend. Is he just **talking through his hat**?
   他到處跟人說美國總統是他的好朋友，那是信口開河的嗎？

2. Don't pay attention to Jack. He was **talking through his hat** when he said he would travel around the world this summer.
   別理傑克了，他說今年夏天會去環遊世界，那只是信口開河而已。

妙語連場

A: Amanda is absent again?

B: She said her grandma was very sick.

A: She was just talking through her hat. Last time, she said her grandpa was very sick, but that's not true.

多學一點

- brag (v.) 吹噓

- lie (v.) 說謊

hear through the grapevine

道聽途說

30

指那些沒有根據，未經證實，而且不可信的消息。

1. Ken **heard through the grapevine** that the final examination would be cancelled.
   阿健道聽途説，以為期末考試將會取消。

2. I **heard through the grapevine** that we're having a new class teacher – is it true?
   聽説我們會有一位新的班主任，這是真的嗎？

妙語連場

A: Do you know that we'll have a transfer student in our class?

B: No, I don't. How do you know that?

A: I heard it from some classmates.

B: Oh, so you heard through the grapevine.

多學一點

- fact (n.) 事實、真相

- ascertain (v.) 弄清楚

指基本的簡單飲食，也可用來形容人們儉樸的生活。

1. If I had to do something bad to make big money, I'd rather **live on bread and water**.
   我寧可過着粗茶淡飯的生活，也不要為了賺錢而去做壞事。

2. My family had to **live on bread and water** when Dad used all his savings to start his business.
   爸爸花光積蓄開拓自己的生意，當時我們一家只能過着粗茶淡飯的日子。

妙語連場

A: What happened to Jason?

B: He was laid off last month.

A: That's too bad... I'm afraid he has to live on bread and water for some time.

多學一點

- survive (v.) 生存

- essential (adj.) 必要的

in one's blood 與生俱來

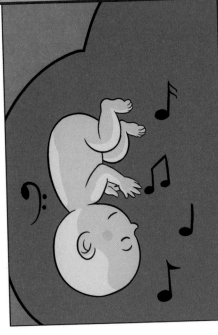

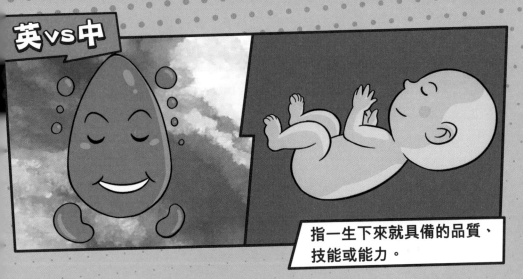

指一生下來就具備的品質、
技能或能力。

1. Sandy is a talented pianist and it's **in her blood** – both her parents are musicians.
   珊迪是一位很有才華的鋼琴家，這是與生俱來的，畢竟她父母都是音樂家。

2. His kindness to stray animals is **in his blood** that he has set up a shelter for them.
   他天生對流浪動物充滿善心，這讓他成立了動物收容所。

妙語連場

Ⓐ: Pam plays tennis very well. Does she practise a lot?

Ⓑ: No, she doesn't. It's in her blood.

Ⓐ: She can be a pro if she is properly trained.

多學一點

- innate (adj.) 天生的

- inherit (v.) 遺傳所得

cry over spilt milk 覆水難收

36

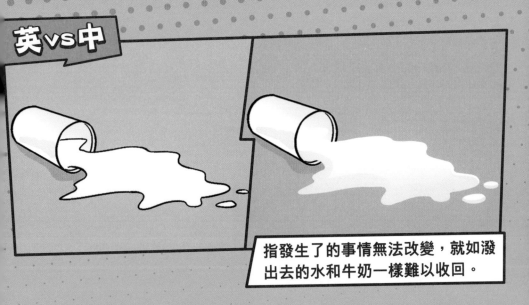

指發生了的事情無法改變，就如潑出去的水和牛奶一樣難以收回。

1. You should fix the problem instead of crying over spilt milk.
   覆水難收，你與其在這裏自怨自艾，還不如解決問題。

2. What is done is done; it's no use crying over spilt milk.
   事情已經發生了，為此難過是沒有用的。

A: What happened to your face?

B: I forgot to wear sunscreen and got a sunburn. I can't go anywhere.

A: Don't cry over spilt milk. You can put on some soothing cream.

多學一點

- regret (v.) 懊悔

- meaningless (adj.) 沒有意義的

have a ball 樂不可支

形容快樂得不得了，參加舞會當然是一件快樂的事！

1. I am sure Betty will **have a ball** on her birthday because all of her friends will come.
   比蒂所有朋友都會來參加她的生日會，相信她一定會玩得樂不可支。

2. We should go **having a ball** after the test.
   測驗完結後，我們一定要去盡情狂歡。

A : Did you have a good time at the party yesterday?

B : Yes, we had a ball.

A : That's great.

多學一點

- mood (n.) 心情

- delighted (adj.) 感到欣喜的

- awesome (adj.) 令人讚歎的

put the cart before the horse 本末倒置

形容做事的次序錯了，或把事物的主次顛倒了。

1. Macy is **putting the cart before the horse** by planning how to spend the pocket money before getting it.
   美詩還未得到零用錢便在想怎樣花這些錢，真是本末倒置。

2. Starving yourself for weight loss is **putting the cart before the horse**. Don't do this again.
   讓自己捱餓來減少重量是本末倒置，你不要再這樣做了。

妙語連場

(A): Why is the stove turned on?

(B): I'm going to cook some vegetables.

(A): Where are the vegetables?

(B): I haven't washed them yet.

(A): Don't put the cart before the horse. You should get the vegetables ready before turning on the stove.

多學一點

• priority (n.) 優先考慮的事

bite the bullet 咬緊牙關

形容忍受着痛苦，勇敢地面對到底！

1. Jenny **bit the bullet** and finally finished her book report.
   珍妮咬緊牙關，終於把閱讀報告完成了。

2. It's freezing but you still have to **bite the bullet** and take a shower.
   天氣很冷，但你還是要咬緊牙關去洗澡。

妙語連場

A: Hey, it's your turn to give a speech next week.

B: Can someone else do it for me? I am scared of speaking in front of so many people.

A: Sorry, you'll just have to bite the bullet.

多學一點

- hurt (v.) 感到疼痛、受傷

- endure (v.) 忍受

- Keep it up!（鼓勵）繼續努力！

the elephant in the room

形容人説話時刻意不理會某些棘手的問題。

1. The fact that my sister failed the exam is **the elephant in the room**.

   對於姐姐考試不合格一事，大家都避而不談。

2. No one wants to bring up **the elephant in the room** about Zoey losing her puppy.

   大家都裝作不知道蘇怡的小狗死了，沒有人想提起這件事。

妙語連場

Ⓐ: Did you know he was lying?

Ⓑ: Yes.

Ⓐ: Why didn't you tell me?

Ⓑ: Well, it's the elephant in the room.

多學一點

- pretend (v.) 假裝
- fake (adj.) 假的

have one's head in the clouds / 神不守舍

形容人心神不定，像在發白日夢一樣。

1. Billy **has his head in the clouds** while his teammates are trying to win the spelling game.
   當一眾隊友在拼字比賽中盡力獲勝時，比利卻神不守舍。

2. Kelly always **has her head in the clouds** in class.
   嘉莉上課時總是神不守舍的。

妙語連場

A : What would you like for lunch?

B : Yes, sure.

A : What? You have your head in the clouds!

多學一點

- daydream (n.) 白日夢

- unaware (adj.) 沒有為意的

- absent-minded (adj.) 心不在焉的

the pot calling the kettle black

五十步笑百步

形容自己跟別人有同樣的錯誤或缺點，
卻因自己的程度較輕而取笑別人。

1. Andy doesn't help with any housework and he says I am lazy. Talk about **the pot calling the kettle black**.
安迪一點家務也不做，卻說我很懶惰，簡直是五十步笑百步。

2. It is a case of **the pot calling the kettle black** when we blame each other – we are both responsible for the project.
我們一同負責這個專題研習，互相指責根本是五十步笑百步。

妙語連場

A: You should go outside and do some exercise instead of sitting all day.

B: Good idea. Shall we go jogging together?

A: Um… It's too hot out there.

B: You're the pot calling the kettle black.

多學一點

- fault (n.) 過失

- equally (adv.) 同樣地

the icing on the cake 錦上添花

This is the best cake in the world.

This is the best scarf in the world.

But what makes it even better?

The icing on the cake!

The embroidery on the scarf!

形容好上加好，美上加美，喜上加喜。

1. The concert is great; the souvenirs for the audience are **the icing on the cake**.
   這場音樂會很精彩，送給觀眾的紀念品更是錦上添花。

2. Cameron is excited to get a place at university – an opportunity to study overseas for one year is **the icing on the cake**.
   卡梅倫為上大學感到十分高興，有機會在國外留學一年更是錦上添花。

A: Thank you for coming to my party, Debbie.

B: This gift is for you. Happy birthday.

A: Oh! It's the icing on the cake.

多學一點

- extra (adj.) 額外的

- enhance (v.) 提升、加強

指沒有直接說明，但在說話裏或字裏行間透露意思。

1. Mom said it's okay. But if you read between the lines, she actually didn't agree with Dad.
   媽媽說沒問題，但你仔細聽她的弦外之音，就知道她並不同意爸爸的話。

2. Amanda is a reserved girl. If you want to get to know her, you need to read between the lines.
   阿曼達是個內向的女孩，如果你想了解她，就要細心解讀她真正的想法。

妙語連場

A: After weeks of not speaking to each other, Doris and Candy finally made peace.

B: I don't think so.

A: But they are chatting about the weather.

B: Read between the lines – they're just pretending.

多學一點

• hidden (adj.) 隱藏的

cut to the chase 開門見山

A monster opened the door...

Then it stepped into the house...

After that, it walked through the room...

Oh, come on! Cut to the chase.

Hey! I'm the mountain monster.

表示直截了當，不轉彎抹角。

1. I am in a rush, so please **cut to the chase** and tell me what you want.

   我趕時間，你想怎樣，請開門見山告訴我。

2. You broke Dad's phone. You should **cut to the chase** and tell him instead of making excuses.

   你把爸爸的電話弄壞了，好應該直接告訴他，而不是找藉口。

妙語連場

A: Hey Peter, I know you are a helpful friend.

B: Let's cut to the chase.

A: I didn't pay attention in class. Can you show me how to do the homework?

多學一點

- impatient (adj.) 沒耐性的

- long-winded (adj.) 長篇大論的

- directly (adv.) 直接地

catch (somebody) on the wrong foot 措手不及

形容來不及應付和處理的情況。

1. Miss Wong gave us a pop quiz today and it **caught us on the wrong foot**.

   黃老師給我們一個突擊測驗，令我們都措手不及。

2. The mom was **caught on the wrong foot** by the baby vomiting suddenly.

   小寶寶突然嘔吐，令那位媽媽措手不及。

A: I'm sorry that I gave you a broken microphone.

B: It's okay. But it totally caught me on the wrong foot when I was giving the speech.

多學一點

- unprepared (adj.) 沒有準備的

- expect (v.) 預料

- surprised (adj.) 感到意外的

knock one's socks off

It's gonna* knock their socks off!

* "gonna" 是 "going to" 的
非正式用法。

指以新的眼光來看待事物。

1. This troupe is very popular and its performance will definitely **knock your socks off**.
   這個劇團十分著名，他們的表演必定令你刮目相看。

2. He is my favourite writer. His latest adventure story totally **knocks my socks off**.
   他是我最喜歡的作家，他最新的冒險故事令我十分驚喜。

Ⓐ: Come, look at this robot.

Ⓑ: Wow, it's awesome!

Ⓐ: It totally knocks your socks off, doesn't it?

多學一點

- 其他說法：blow one's socks off

- impress (v.) 令人留下深刻印象

- fascinating (adj.) 吸引人的

let the cat out of the bag 露出馬腳

They are my new friends –

Kitty and Pony.

They look strange...

Hi!

英vs中

指無意間暴露出不願別人知道的真相或漏洞。

1. Ellen has finally **let the cat out of the bag** after all the lies she told.
   愛倫謊話連篇，最後終於露出馬腳。

2. We want to give Candy a surprise on her birthday, so don't **let the cat out of the bag**.
   我們想給凱蒂一個生日驚喜，你可別把風聲洩露出去啊。

妙語連場

(A): Mom found out that we'd bought the new game.

(B): How so? Did we let the cat out of the bag?

(A): We left the receipt on the table.

多學一點

- reveal (v.) 揭露

- clue (n.) 線索

- secret (n.) 秘密

put oneself in somebody's shoes 將心比心

Oh poor girl, I'll buy all of your matches.

Thank you! If you want to know me more...

Why don't you put yourself in my shoes?

stink!

設想自己處在與別人相同的情況，去為別人考慮。

1. It took Sam a few weeks to build this model ship. If you **put yourself in his shoes**, you would understand why he doesn't want anyone to touch it.
   阿森花了幾星期才砌好這艘模型船，要是你能將心比心，便會理解他為什麼不願意別人觸碰它。

2. Teddy is a popular counsellor because he always **puts himself in his students' shoes** and gives the best advice.
   托迪是一位受歡迎的輔導員，因為他總會將心比心去考慮學生的情況，給予最好的建議。

妙語連場

A: My grandma has been so grumpy since she moved into the nursing home.

B: Put yourself in her shoes, you'd understand she may feel lonely.

A: You're right. I will go visit her tomorrow.

多學一點

- empathise (v.) 產生共鳴、表示同情

形容把不重要的小事當作大事來處理，有故意誇張的意思。

1. Don't pay attention to Jenny. She always makes a storm in a teacup over tiny issues.
   別理珍妮，她經常小題大做。

2. Benny and Chris are good friends. I am sure their disagreement is just a storm in a teacup.
   賓尼和克里斯是好朋友，我相信他們的分歧只是小問題。

A : Why are there so many people at the supermarket?

B : They are stockpiling food because of the typhoon.

A : They are making a storm in a teacup! The typhoon is not hitting here.

多學一點

- 其他說法：tempest in a teapot

- trivial (adj.) 微不足道的

- exaggerate (v.) 誇大

run round like a headless chicken 手忙腳亂

66

形容忙着做很多事情，以致做事慌亂，沒有條理。

1. He is now **running round like a headless chicken** while making breakfast for his mom.
   他正在為媽媽煮早餐，弄得手忙腳亂。

2. We have to make sure everything is ready for the school open day tomorrow so that we won't **run round like a headless chicken**.
   我們必須確保一切準備就緒，以免明天學校開放日時大家會手忙腳亂。

妙語連場

A: Why are you still sitting here? You should start packing your bag.

B: Relax. We still have time.

A: Start packing now or you will run round like a headless chicken.

多學一點

- uncontrolled (adj.) 失控的

- haste (n.) 倉促

broaden one's horizons

大開眼界

I have a craving for knowledge.

I read many books.

And I turn my head 270 degrees around.

It hurts, but it broadens my horizons.

形容大大地增長知識，增廣見聞。

1. Travelling is one of the best ways to broaden your horizons.
   旅行是其中一種讓你大開眼界的好方法。

2. There are many benefits of volunteering. Helping people make you happy; it also broadens your horizons, too.
   做義工有很多好處：幫助別人不僅能令你快樂，更會擴闊你的視野。

妙語連場

Ⓐ : I visited the Art Museum with my family last week.

Ⓑ : Is it worth a visit?

Ⓐ : Absolutely. It contains a lot of masterpieces that will broaden your horizons.

多學一點

- 其他說法：widen one's horizons

- expand (v.) 擴大、增加

- curious (adj.) 好奇的

hit the ceiling 怒髮衝冠

No more fighting, or you will be punished.

!?

You can't hit me.

I am hitting the ceiling!

形容非常憤怒的樣子。

1. Mom **hit the ceiling** when she found out I didn't tidy up my room.
   我沒有把房間收拾好，媽媽氣得怒髮衝冠。

2. Tommy will **hit the ceiling** if his request is rejected.
   如果湯米的要求被拒絕的話，他會氣得怒髮衝冠。

妙語連場

A: Why didn't you come to the rehearsal yesterday?

B: I completely forgot it. Was Miss Chan mad?

A: She hit the ceiling. I think you are out.

多學一點

- 其他説法：hit the roof

- furious (adj.) 怒不可遏的

- calm (adj.) 鎮定的

- Keep your temper. 不要發脾氣。

71

poles apart 天壤之別

英vs中

形容差別極大，就像南北兩極或天與地一樣完全不同。

1. Though Tommy and William are twins, their personalities are poles apart.
   雖然湯米和偉林是孿生兄弟，他們的性格卻有天壤之別。

2. Our views are poles apart, but we should respect each other.
   即使我們的看法截然不同，也應該要彼此尊重。

妙語連場

Ⓐ: How is your secondary school life?

Ⓑ: It's poles apart from the primary school. We have many subjects to study now.

Ⓐ: Sounds challenging!

多學一點

- completely (adv.) 徹底地

- opposite (adj.) 相反的、不同的

73

back to square one 捲土重來

形容失敗之後重新再來一遍。

1. Mom failed the driving test last year. This year, she is **back to square one** and retakes the driving test.
   媽媽去年考取駕駛執照失敗，今年她捲土重來，再次報考。

2. If you misread the essay topic, you may have to go **back to square one**.
   寫文章時，如果你審錯了題目，就可能要把文章從頭再寫。

A: Our plan didn't work.

B: What can we do?

A: I'm afraid we're back to square one.

多學一點

- attempt (v.) 嘗試

- return (v.) 返回

- all over again 重頭再來

你想知道嗎？

I like fishing in troubled waters.
請翻閱第 94–95 頁。

魚類的敵人

My life is just a chapter of accidents...
請翻閱第 104–105 頁。

不幸的小孩

Every time I cast a spell, I get tongue-tied...
請翻閱第 78–79 頁。

說不出咒語的魔女

No one wants this hot potato...
請翻閱第 82–83 頁。

被人嫌棄的小薯

文化共通篇

雖然中西文化各不相同，
有些成語卻會巧合地使用相同的文字來表達！

形容人因為害怕或緊張，使舌頭像打了結一樣，張開嘴巴卻說不出話來。

1. Derek got **tongue-tied** when his teacher asked him to answer the question.
   當老師問戴力問題時，戴力顯得張口結舌。

2. I was so nervous and **tongue-tied** in the interview.
   面試時，我緊張得張口結舌。

妙語連場

A: I think Paul was the one who broke the globe.

B: Why do you think so?

A: He got so tongue-tied when Mr. Chan asked him about it.

多學一點

- flustered (adj.) 慌張的

- express (v.) 表達

- speechless (adj.) 啞口無言的

79

kill two birds with one stone 一石二鳥

Enough is enough!

形容做一件事情，達到了兩個目的。

1. Reading English comics **kills two birds with one stone**. It's entertaining and you can learn conversational English.
閱讀英文漫畫既有趣，又能學習英文口語，真是一石二鳥。

2. Mom is going to the post office and she will pick up the groceries on the way back, **killing two birds with one stone**.
媽媽要去郵局，回來時順道去買東西，真是一舉兩得。

妙語連場

A: Oh, you bring your own lunch?

B: Yes, it's healthier and it costs me less.

A: Nice! It kills two birds with one stone.

多學一點

- effective (adj.) 有效的

- purpose (n.) 目的

- at a time 每次

hot potato 烫手山芋

82

英 vs 中

指難辦得大家都不願意接手的
事情，或難以處置的東西。

1. Global warming is a **hot potato** that many countries don't want to touch.
   很多國家都不願碰「全球暖化」這燙手山芋。

2. Matthew dropped the plan like a **hot potato** when he knew it was not workable.
   當麥菲知道他的計劃行不通後，這計劃隨即成了燙手山芋，擱置下來。

妙語連場

A : Brian becomes the new coach of the football team. Good luck to him.

B : Oh?

A : The boys are very disobedient and nobody wants to touch that hot potato.

多學一點

- complex (adj.) 複雜難懂的

- handle (v.) 處理

save (something) for a rainy day 未雨綢繆

形容預先做好準備，防患未然。

1. Mom and Dad always **save** a portion of their salaries each month **for a rainy day**.
   爸爸媽媽每月都會把工資一部分存起，未雨綢繆。

2. My grandpa gave me money as my birthday gift. I'll **save** it **for a rainy day**.
   我生日時，爺爺給我錢作禮物。我會把這些錢存起來，以備不時之需。

妙語連場

A: My computer was broken but I can't afford a new one.

B: You get your pocket money every week.

A: I've bought some new games.

B: You should start saving some money for a rainy day.

多學一點

- waste (v.) 浪費

- foresee (v.) 預見、預知

add fuel to the fire

火上加油

英 vs 中

表示讓事態變得更加嚴重，或使人更加生氣。

1. Don't yell at Mom; it will only **add fuel to the fire**.
   不要呼喝媽媽，這只會火上加油。

2. It would **add fuel to the fire** if I told her the truth.
   如果我把真相告訴她，恐怕只會火上加油。

妙語連場

A: She is so mad now. You should stay away from her.

B: But I want to apologise.

A: Don't add fuel to the fire.

多學一點

- worsen (v.) 使情況惡化

- douse (v.) 澆熄

- inflame (v.) 激起

- tense (adj.) 令人緊張的

形容人羞愧、尷尬、焦急或發怒時的樣子。

1. Samuel was **red in the face** when he heard people laughing at him.
   當森美聽到身邊的人取笑他時,他不禁面紅耳赤起來。

2. Tommy became **red in the face** when Mom was telling the teacher that he had wet the bed last night.
   媽媽把湯米昨晚尿牀的事告訴了老師,令湯米頓時面紅耳赤。

妙語連場

Ⓐ: Martha couldn't help yawning during the lesson.

Ⓑ: That's hilarious!

Ⓐ: Miss Chan was red in the face.

多學一點

- embarrass (v.) 令人感到尷尬

- ashamed (adj.) 難為情的

- stomp (v.) 生氣地跺腳

have a heart of stone 鐵石心腸

形容內心殘忍得像堅固的石頭一樣硬，不為感情所動。

1. Candy says I **have a heart of stone** because I never cry when I see sad movies.
   凱蒂説我是個鐵石心腸的人，因為我看悲情的電影時從來不哭。

2. Don't ask Daniel to volunteer for anything. He **has a heart of stone**.
   別邀請丹尼爾參與任何義務工作了，他是一個鐵石心腸的人。

妙語連場

A: You look so tired. Are you okay?

B: I didn't sleep well because my baby brother kept crying all night long. Do you think Mr. Chan would allow me to skip the PE lesson today?

A: I don't think so. He has a heart of stone.

多學一點

- cruel (adj.) 殘忍的

- sympathy (n.) 同情心

plain sailing 一帆風順

英VS中

指事情非常順利，沒有任何阻礙。

1. He is a successful businessman now, but it hasn't been always **plain sailing**.
   他現在是一位成功的商人，但他的事業並非從一開始就一帆風順。

2. We are doing the final check on the camping equipment to make sure the trip will be **plain sailing**.
   為確保行程順利，我們最後再檢查一遍露營的設備。

妙語連場

Ⓐ: Denise was defeated by the newbie in the chess tournament.

Ⓑ: It's unexpected! She'd won for a few times.

Ⓐ: Maybe it's good for her to know that life is not always plain sailing.

多學一點

- 其他說法：smooth sailing

- ups and downs (n.) 起跌浮沉

fish in troubled waters

渾水摸魚

We have trouble here. The water is getting mucky.

Don't fish in troubled waters!

指趁着情況混亂時，從中獲取利益。

1. That man wanted to **fish in troubled waters** by stealing things while the owner was clearing up the shop after the flood.
   店主正在清理下雨時湧進店內的積水，那人竟然想渾水摸魚偷東西。

2. If you are really his friend, you shouldn't **fish in troubled waters** by lending money at high rates of interest to him.
   如果你是他真正的朋友，就不應該渾水摸魚，借錢給他卻收取高利息。

妙語連場

Ⓐ : Whenever I do something wrong and get caught by my mom, my little brother will fish in troubled waters.

Ⓑ : What will he do?

Ⓐ : He will act nice and then ask for an ice cream.

多學一點

- advantage (n.) 好處

- cunning (adj.) 狡猾的

on thin ice 如履薄冰

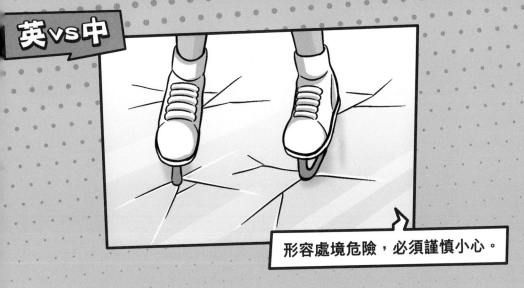

英vs中

形容處境危險，必須謹慎小心。

1. In ancient times, serving an emperor was like skating **on thin ice** that no mistakes were allowed.
在古時候，侍奉皇帝如履薄冰，不容有半點差錯。

2. Derek is **on thin ice** by copying his friend's homework.
德力冒着風險抄他朋友的功課。

妙語連場

Ⓐ : Mom told me you got very good marks in your test. She was so happy.

Ⓑ : I lied about it. I didn't want to upset her.

Ⓐ : You are on thin ice.

多學一點

- precarious (adj.) 不穩固的
- vulnerable (adj.) 脆弱的
- at risk 處境危險

If we get good marks, we will...

If we have meat for dinner, we will...

形容高興得雙手起舞，兩腳跳動。

1. The students won the contest and they were **dancing in the streets**.
   同學們勝出了比賽，興奮得手舞足蹈。

2. The parents are **dancing in the streets** about their baby taking his first steps.
   小寶寶剛會走路了，他的父母都高興得手舞足蹈。

妙語連場

A: Martha got the scholarship to study abroad.

B: She must be dancing in the streets.

A: Yes, she had worked very hard on it.

多學一點

- ecstatic (adj.) 欣喜若狂

- pleasure (n.) 歡樂

- have a ball 樂不可支（請翻閱第 38-39 頁。）

have one's number

心中有數

指摸清某個人的底細，清楚知道那人的行動。（「心中有數」可以指對人或事情，但 have one's number 專指人。）

1. Don't ever try to fool Mom. She **has your number**; she knows you don't like carrots and she will check the bin.
   不要嘗試欺騙媽媽，她可是心中有數。她知道你不喜歡吃紅蘿蔔，一定會去檢查垃圾桶（看你有沒有丟掉）。

2. I know how to beat his team. I **have their number**.
   我對他那隊人非常了解，知道怎樣可以打敗他們。

妙語連場

A: What's going on?

B: Peter lost the game and asked us to leave him alone.

A: Let me talk to him. I have his number.

多學一點

- anticipate (v.) 預期、預料

- understand (v.) 理解

101

turn a blind eye 視而不見

英vs中

指明明睜着眼睛看，卻什麼也沒有見到。

1. Parents should not **turn a blind eye** to their kids' dishonest behaviour.
父母不應對孩子不誠實的行為視而不見。

2. We should never **turn a blind eye** to animal cruelty.
我們不應對虐待動物視而不見。

妙語連場

A: I get bullied by some classmates.

B: You should tell Miss Wong.

A: But they are her favourite students.

B: She is a righteous person; she won't turn a blind eye to it.

多學一點

- knowingly (adv.) 知情地、故意地

- connive (v.) 默許、縱容

- face up to 正視

Life is a tragedy!

英VS中

指禍患接二連三地發生。

1. It was **a chapter of accidents** that my cousin lost his job and got a bad disease.
我的表哥不僅失業了，還患上了嚴重的疾病，真是禍不單行。

2. Our picnic day ended up as **a chapter of accidents** when Jason lost his bag and Mia fell off the bike.
祖信的袋不見了，美雅又從單車上摔下來，結果我們的野餐日演變成一連串災禍。

妙語連場

Ⓐ : The cruise trip was a chapter of accidents.

Ⓑ : What happened?

Ⓐ : My mom was seasick most of the time and my dad had diarrhoea.

多學一點

• mishap (n.) 厄運、不幸事故

• unlucky (adj.) 不幸的

come rain or shine 風雨無阻

形容無論什麼情況都會照常進行，颱風下雨也阻擋不了。

1. Mrs Wong goes swimming at 6 am every morning, **come rain or shine**.
   黃太太每天早上 6 時都會去游泳，風雨無阻。

2. My dad takes me to football training every Saturday, **come rain or shine**.
   爸爸逢星期六都會帶我去參加足球訓練，風雨無阻。

妙語連場

A: Don't forget our party tomorrow.

B: But the forecast says it will rain tomorrow.

A: Come rain or shine, the party will start on time.

多學一點

- determined (adj.) 堅定的

- anyway (adv.) 無論如何

- whatever (pron.) 不管怎樣

成語實戰賽

看看以下各題的着色部分，然後從框內選出可以用哪一句來表達出同樣的意思，把代表字母填在空格內。

A. see the light

B. Time flies

C. cry over spilt milk

D. having a ball

E. the icing on the cake

F. read between the lines

G. knocked our socks off

H. broadens my horizons

1. It's useless to **waste time feeling sorry**! ☐

2. I believe you will finally **realise how to solve the problem** if you keep trying. ☐

3. The concert **was very impressive**! ☐

4. **Time seems to pass very quickly**! It's almost time to go home. ☐

5. The zoo is amazing! Its workshop for children is **an extra good thing**. ☐

6. The kids are **having so much fun** in the party. ☐

7. If you **understand what she really means**, you will know she is actually very proud of you. ☐

8. The current exhibition held in the art gallery totally **expands my knowledge**. ☐

看看以下各題的着色部分，然後從書中選出可以用哪一句來表達出同樣的意思，填在橫線上。

1. **Whatever the weather**, we won't cancel the show.

2. Tammy was **so embarrassed** that she got into the wrong room.

3. If you don't want to **make it worse**, you should immediately tell the truth.

4. The lucky draw winner got ten thousand cash and he was **extremely happy**.

5. Pansy is very detail-minded. The event will be **smooth** under her supervision.

6. Samuel was daydreaming while Ms. Chan was teaching the new topic. When Ms. Chan asked him to answer the question, he was **speechless**.

答案

1. C
2. A
3. G
4. B
5. E
6. D
7. F
8. H

1. Come rain or shine

2. red in the face

3. add fuel to the fire

4. dancing in the streets

5. plain sailing

6. tongue-tied

趣味漫畫學英語

中英成語有文化
Idioms and Phrases

作　　　者：Elaine Tin
插　　　圖：岑卓華
責任編輯：林沛暘
美術設計：蔡學彰
出　　　版：新雅文化事業有限公司
　　　　　　香港英皇道 499 號北角工業大廈 18 樓
　　　　　　電話：(852) 2138 7998
　　　　　　傳真：(852) 2597 4003
　　　　　　網址：http://www.sunya.com.hk
　　　　　　電郵：marketing@sunya.com.hk
發　　　行：香港聯合書刊物流有限公司
　　　　　　香港荃灣德士古道 220-248 號荃灣工業中心 16 樓
　　　　　　電話：(852) 2150 2100
　　　　　　傳真：(852) 2407 3062
　　　　　　電郵：info@suplogistics.com.hk
印　　　刷：中華商務彩色印刷有限公司
　　　　　　香港新界大埔汀麗路 36 號
版　　　次：二〇二〇年八月初版
　　　　　　二〇二四年四月第五次印刷

ISBN: 978-962-08-7562-5
© 2020 Sun Ya Publications (HK) Ltd.
18/F, North Point Industrial Building, 499 King's Road, Hong Kong
Published in Hong Kong SAR, China
Printed in China